THE ORPHANS OF THE AMAZON

ABHIRAJ GUPTA

BlueRose ONE.com
Stories Matter
NewDelhi • London

BLUEROSE PUBLISHERS
India | U.K.

BlueRose ONE.com
Stories Matter
NewDelhi • London

For permissions requests or inquiries regarding this publication, please contact:

BLUEROSE PUBLISHERS
www.BlueRoseONE.com
info@bluerosepublishers.com
+91 8882 898 898
+4407342408967

ISBN: 978-93-7542-399-7

Cover design: Yash Singhal
Typesetting: Namrata Saini

First Edition: February 2026

Acknowledgement

Thanks to my mom and dad for supporting me. Thanks to my family and friends for helping me write my first book. I also thank all my teachers for motivating me to achieve this major accomplishment. I also thank the people who buy this book and the reviewers of this book.

Contents

Chapter 1
The Introduction

Joseph shook his sleepy friend, Tercia, awake.

"Wake up! It's already 9:00 AM," he said.

Breakfast at the orphanage was always served at 9:15 AM, and anyone who hadn't showered and brushed their teeth wasn't allowed to eat. Rushing through his morning routine, Joseph quickly used some toothpaste, gargled, and took a shower.

Tercia and Joseph always sat together at breakfast. They were good friends but often got bullied for their appearance. Most of the orphans were of Brazilian origin and excellent football players, while Tercia and Joseph, of South Asian descent, were known for their intelligence, particularly in science. The orphanage was located in the city of Manaus, near the mighty Amazon rainforest.

As they reached the buffet, a group of bullies approached them, teasing them as usual. Joseph, fed up with the constant harassment, finally snapped. Without thinking, he punched one of the three bullies square in the face, sparking a brawl. Tercia quickly called the warden and reported the incident. As punishment, the bullies were made to fast for an entire day. Tercia and Joseph laughed at the outcome, unaware of what awaited them.

After breakfast, which consisted of a cheese sandwich and a bowl of cereal with milk, they spent their time reading their favorite encyclopedia about dinosaurs and survival tactics in harsh environments. Later, they played tag with friends, though they weren't great at running and got caught almost every time. Exhausted, they drank nearly two liters of water before heading to bed.

However, the bullies weren't done with them. They set up a prank using water balloons, rigging them above the door. As soon as Tercia and Joseph entered their room, the balloons burst, drenching them. The bullies had somehow snuck out of the detention room unnoticed, making it impossible to report them.

Determined to get back at them, Tercia and Joseph devised a plan. They placed a bowl of flour above the detention room door, waiting for their moment. To lure the bullies out, they taunted them, enraging them enough to storm out of the room. As they opened the door wider, the bowl tipped over, covering them in flour. Tercia and Joseph ran off, giggling.

Feeling bored, they played board games until bedtime at 9:30 PM. That night, Tercia felt discomfort but chose not to wake

Joseph. After some time, he fell asleep, assuming it was just a minor ache. The next morning, feeling better, he woke up early and completed his routine before Joseph even stirred. When Joseph finally woke up, he wasn't surprised, knowing Tercia had woken earlier only to go back to sleep.

At breakfast, Tercia hurried through his meal, eager to read a survival book he had bought with his allowance. He devoured thirty pages before taking a midday nap. But as he slept, the bullies snuck into his room, dragged him to the janitor's closet, and beat him viciously. His screams were muffled, but Joseph heard him and rushed to get the warden. Upon discovering Tercia's condition, the warden provided him with first aid, medicine, and a special bed reserved for the sick and injured. Others were jealous of the privilege, but Joseph was only concerned for his friend.

The bullies faced a harsher punishment: five days of starvation, allowed only four liters of water daily. By the next morning, Tercia felt significantly better.

When Joseph checked on him, he was relieved to see his friend recovering. For breakfast, Tercia was given cereals, fruits, and lentils. After some rest, he resumed reading his book, absorbing another twenty-five pages on survival techniques. Eager to test a method for making fire with stones, he asked Joseph to try it for him. Joseph obliged, and to their excitement, it worked! Inspired, they decided to attempt more survival experiments within the orphanage.

Chapter 2
The Survival Try-Outs

The rest of the day dragged on. Sitting in class, Joseph tapped his pencil against the desk while pretending to copy notes. Tercia, slumped beside him, kept glancing at the clock.

Neither of them could stop thinking about the little camp they had built—or the bigger idea it sparked.

"Do you think we could survive in a real forest?" Tercia whispered suddenly.

Joseph raised an eyebrow. "You mean, like the *actual* Amazon?"

Tercia nodded, his voice a little lower now. "Yeah. I mean... what if we had to? Not for fun. What if we got stuck there?"

Joseph gave it a second. "I dunno. Maybe? I think we could last a few days. If we had matches and, like, snacks."

Tercia smirked. "That's not survival, that's camping."

They both chuckled, earning a sharp glare from their geography teacher.

Later that evening, they went back to their little "base" behind the kitchen. The fire pit was now cold, a little circle of ash where their excitement had burned earlier. Joseph crouched beside it, tracing a circle in the dirt.

"You know what sucks?" he said suddenly. "That we keep having to *pretend*. Like... we're out here building stuff, but it's still just behind the orphanage. Still just us."

Tercia looked up. "Yeah. I wish it was real too."

There was a short pause, the kind that's not awkward—just quiet.

"I don't even remember my parents," Joseph added, poking at a twig. "I mean, I *know* I had them. But I don't remember their faces. Or their voices."

Tercia sat down next to him. "I remember mine. But... only when I try really hard. Like holding onto a dream that's slipping away."

Neither of them spoke after that for a while. The sky above them turned a soft orange, birds calling in the distance. The moment felt big, somehow.

Then Joseph stood up and said, "Wanna build a water trap?"

Tercia laughed. "That's the most Joseph thing you could've said right now."

"What? We're trying to survive, aren't we?"

They spent the next hour experimenting with a system to catch rainwater using old plastic bottles and bits of wire.

It didn't work perfectly—most of the water leaked out—but they didn't care. They were learning. Failing. Figuring it out. And that felt real.

Before bedtime, they lay on the grass, their heads resting on bundled-up jackets.

"You think we'll ever leave this place?" Joseph asked quietly.

Tercia was quiet for a moment. "I don't know. But I think if we ever do... we'll be ready."

Chapter 3
Preparation for Wisdom

The week after their survival experiments, Joseph and Tercia's minds were consumed by one thing: the Amazon rainforest. It wasn't just a far-off dream anymore; it was something *real* they could do. Something they could achieve. They were going to survive in it. Together.

It started as a passing comment during one of their many late-night talks.

"Imagine actually going there," Joseph had said, tossing a paper airplane toward the ceiling. "Just... living there, in the middle of the Amazon, like explorers or something."

Tercia had looked up from his survival book, where he was reading about poisonous plants. "What if we could?" he said, his voice low but filled with a spark Joseph hadn't expected. "What if we actually tried?"

Joseph had paused, the idea settling in his mind like a stone sinking into water. "You mean... really go? Like, leave the orphanage?"

Tercia grinned. "Why not? We know survival skills now. We could make it."

Joseph had laughed nervously at first. "We're kids. We're orphans. No one's going to let us run off into the Amazon."

But Tercia wasn't joking. He sat up, his eyes shining with an idea that Joseph hadn't seen before. "We don't have to just leave. We can *prepare.* Start small. Gather everything we need. And then... I don't know, find a way."

The more they talked about it, the more Joseph's doubt faded. The idea felt like a flame spreading—first small, but now warming their entire world. Why not? They had survived the orphanage, didn't they? Surviving the Amazon felt like the next step.

By the next morning, they were already planning.

Step 1: Do the Research

Tercia's books about survival had already taught them some basic techniques, but the Amazon was unlike any environment they'd ever imagined. They needed more than just fire-starting methods—they needed real knowledge. Real wisdom.

They began raiding the orphanage library, pulling out every book they could find about the rainforest. They Googled everything they could on the orphanage computer, even though the connection was slow and unreliable. They asked their teachers for advice. Ms. Joans, their biology teacher, gave them a list of plants and animals they'd likely encounter, explaining what to avoid and what could be useful.

"Be careful of the venomous frogs," she warned. "But also, there are some medicinal plants you could use."

It was like every day they discovered something new, some tidbit of information that made the dream seem more possible.

Step 2: The Gear

The next challenge was gear. Neither of them had money to buy high-tech survival equipment. So they got creative.

Joseph dug through old boxes of camping supplies in the orphanage storeroom, finding an old, rusted knife, a weathered tarp, and a half-melted flashlight. The knife was barely usable, but it would have to do. The flashlight barely worked, but it could be recharged by shaking it. Tercia, with his clever hands, worked on fixing things, repairing the tarp with needle and thread, making sure it would hold together in a downpour. They managed to find a few old bottles, perfect for collecting rainwater, and even an old compass, which seemed like the most important tool of all.

"I think we need to be prepared for every situation," Joseph said, packing the items into an old backpack. "This could be dangerous. We can't underestimate the rainforest."

"I'm not underestimating it," Tercia replied, tightening the straps on his own backpack. "But I think we're ready. The more we prepare, the more we can handle whatever comes."

Step 3: Physical Training

They hadn't even thought about it at first—how would their bodies hold up in the wild? The Amazon was *huge*. The humidity was relentless. The terrain was unforgiving. They needed to be in shape, but the orphanage gym wasn't exactly the place to train for a jungle expedition.

Instead, they ran laps around the orphanage, doing push-ups and sit-ups during their breaks. They'd run into the nearby forest for short "trials," climbing trees and crawling under bushes, pretending they were on a scouting mission.

One morning, they woke up early, before the others, and ran through the streets of Manaus. The hot, humid air wrapped around them, making their skin sticky, but they kept going.

"Ready for this?" Tercia asked, breathless.

Joseph wiped his forehead. "I think we have no choice."

They both laughed, even though deep down, they knew this wasn't going to be easy. It was going to be grueling, exhausting—and they were scared.

Step 4: Overcoming Doubts

In the evenings, when they lay in bed exhausted from their physical training and their growing sense of responsibility, Joseph would sometimes question the entire idea.

"Maybe we're not cut out for this," he said one night, his voice a little shaky. "What if something happens? What if we're not strong enough? What if we get lost?"

Tercia turned on his side, eyes serious but calm. "We *are* strong enough. We just have to believe that we are. Everyone starts somewhere, right?"

Joseph nodded, his stomach flipping with a mix of excitement and fear.

"You think the Amazon's ready for us?" he asked, a hint of humor in his voice.

Tercia's eyes flickered with something fierce. "I think *we're* ready for it."

The idea of leaving the orphanage, leaving behind everything they knew, had started to feel more like a necessity. They needed to do this. Not just for themselves, but to prove something—to show that even orphans could be strong enough, clever enough, to survive.

A Few Days Later

The two friends stood in front of the orphanage gates, backpacks strapped tight, hearts pounding with a mixture of excitement and fear. The jungle was just beyond the gates of the city. It was real now. They were actually going.

"I'm scared," Joseph admitted, his voice quiet.

Tercia smiled, a grin that was half confidence, half nervousness. "We're going to make it."

As the gates of the orphanage loomed behind them, they took a step forward, together.

The jungle awaited.

Chapter 4
Arrival and Survival

The Amazon rainforest was nothing like the pictures in their books or the grainy videos they'd seen online. It was bigger, louder, more alive. The air was thick, buzzing with the sounds of insects and distant birdcalls. Sunlight streamed through gaps in the canopy like golden waterfalls, illuminating the vibrant greens all around them.

Joseph and Tercia stood still for a moment, taking it all in. Their boots sunk slightly into the damp earth as they adjusted their backpacks. It had taken them two full days of walking from the city outskirts, navigating muddy trails and crossing small streams. They had gotten lost—twice—but managed to find their way again thanks to the compass and Tercia's uncanny sense of direction.

"I think this is it," Tercia said, finally stopping at a small clearing surrounded by tall trees. Right in the center stood a large fruit tree, its branches drooping with bright orange berries neither of them recognized, but which smelled sweet and looked safe.

Joseph wiped his forehead and let out a long breath. "We made it."

They dropped their bags and plopped onto the ground, laughing—not out of humor, but relief. The moment felt unreal. They were really here. In the Amazon. On their own.

Setting Up Camp

First, they cleared the area under the fruit tree of leaves and twigs, making space for their shelter. Using the tarp, long sticks they had collected, and a length of rope, they built a simple A-frame tent. It took them an hour of struggling—figuring out angles, hammering sticks into the soft earth, redoing knots—but eventually, the tent stood strong and neat. It wasn't much, but to them, it looked like a five-star jungle hotel.

They spread out the old bedsheet they'd brought as a base and tucked their water bottles, matches, and the survival guide safely in one corner. The fruit tree above provided both shade and food—although they still planned to test the berries with their survival book before eating anything.

"I can't believe we're actually doing this," Joseph said, as he flopped back onto the ground next to the tent.

"Believe it," Tercia grinned, holding up one of the berries. "Step one of survival: find food. Step two: don't eat it unless you're sure it won't kill you."

They both laughed.

First Meal in the Wild

Using the fire-starting method they'd practiced so many times at the orphanage—flint, stones, and dried leaves—they got a small fire going. Smoke spiraled gently upward as they boiled water in an old tin cup to purify it. Next, they opened a small packet of lentils they had carried and made a basic soup. It tasted bland, but to them, it was the best meal ever. Hunger—and achievement—can make anything delicious.

As night began to fall, the forest changed. The air cooled, and new sounds filled the space—howling monkeys, the distant hoot of an owl, the occasional rustle in the underbrush.

They sat side by side near the fire, listening.

"Do you think anyone's looking for us?" Joseph asked quietly.

"Probably," Tercia replied. "But I think... for the first time, we're doing something that's truly *ours*. We're not just kids in an orphanage anymore. We're... explorers."

Joseph smiled and looked up at the stars peeking through the treetops. "Explorers with a tent under a fruit tree."

"Perfect, right?"

"Perfect."

That night, they crawled into their tent, exhausted but proud. The forest cradled them in its wild arms as they fell asleep to the hum of insects and the rhythm of distant rain dripping off leaves. For the first time in a long time, they felt at peace—not just in their surroundings, but with themselves.

They had arrived.

They had survived their first day.

And they were just getting started.

Chapter 5
How Many Days?

The second morning in the Amazon was both beautiful and brutal. The sunrise cast golden beams through the misty treetops, dew clung to every leaf, and the air smelled like damp bark and moss. But peace didn't last long—because Joseph and Tercia were already knee-deep in an argument.

"I'm telling you—we stay for **a whole month**," Tercia said confidently, balancing on a log with his arms crossed. "Thirty days out here. Living off the land. Real survival."

Joseph turned so fast he nearly spilled the tin cup of boiled water he was holding. "Have you *completely* lost it?"

Tercia shrugged. "Why not? We've got food, we've got gear. We've got knowledge."

"We have *a backpack, a tarp, and two survival books*, Tercia. Not a full Amazon expedition team!"

Tercia hopped off the log and crouched near the fire pit. "Come on, think about it. We'd actually have time to test everything—fire-building, fishing, traps, water purification, even shelter upgrades. A week isn't enough to *master* any of that."

Joseph rubbed his forehead. "We're not here to become wild jungle men! We're still orphans with a curfew and responsibilities. You think the orphanage won't report us missing? You think they'll say, 'Oh, the boys are probably just learning how to survive in the rainforest'?"

Tercia grinned. "Maybe they'll admire our courage."

Joseph shot him a look. "Or send the police."

Tercia picked up a stone and tossed it into the underbrush. "So? They never cared about us before. Always treated us like background noise. At least out here, we're doing something real."

Joseph paused, caught off-guard by that. There was pain under Tercia's words—an ache he knew all too well.

"I get it," Joseph said softly. "But survival isn't just about proving something. It's about *not dying*. And thirty days? That's not survival. That's asking for trouble."

Tercia looked up, about to reply—but a **sudden rustle** cut him off.

From the dense thicket behind their tent came a loud *crack* of branches. Something big was moving. And it wasn't walking. It was **slithering**.

A long, green snake emerged—easily six feet, maybe more. Its head was lifted slightly, tongue flicking the air, eyes unblinking.

Tercia instinctively stepped back. "Don't move," he whispered.

Joseph was already frozen, heart pounding. The snake glided silently across the ground, coming closer, winding its way between them and the tent.

Joseph took a slow, shaky step back—and tripped on a root, falling with a grunt.

The snake snapped its head toward the sound.

Tercia, thinking fast, grabbed a stick and jabbed it near the ground in front of the snake—not to hit it, but to startle it. It worked. The snake hissed, then turned and slipped back into the jungle, disappearing as silently as it had come.

The boys didn't move for a full minute.

Then Joseph finally sat up and whispered, "I almost *died* because of your one-month plan."

Tercia stared at him, then suddenly burst out laughing—half relief, half nerves. "Okay, okay. Maybe thirty days *is* a bit much."

Joseph let out a shaky laugh of his own. "Yeah, I vote for ten. We'll call it the middle ground."

Tercia nodded, wiping sweat from his brow. "Ten it is. Then we'll *re-evaluate*."

They sat there in silence, just breathing. The trees swayed gently, as if pretending nothing had happened. But the moment lingered. That was no prank, no game. That was **real** jungle danger. And it had looked them right in the eye.

Joseph broke the silence. "Still want to be Bear Grylls?"

Tercia smiled. "Maybe... the junior version."

They laughed, this time genuinely, the fear slowly fading. One thing was clear now—they weren't just pretending. They were *really* doing this. And the jungle wasn't going to let them forget it.

Chapter 6
Survival Preparation for the Scary Month

Joseph woke before dawn, every muscle tingling with anticipation. A pale light filtered through the leaves overhead, illuminating the droplets of dew that clung to each frond. He lay perfectly still in the shelter they'd built beneath the great fruit tree, listening to the jungle's waking chorus. Somewhere above, a troupe of monkeys chattered; down below, insects began their eternal symphony. He glanced over at Tercia, who was already sitting up with a small journal and pencil, sketching hastily by the dim beam of a shake-powered headlamp.

"Morning," Tercia whispered, brushing a leaf from his leg. He closed the journal and tucked the pencil behind his ear with a determined nod. Joseph swung his legs over the edge of their makeshift cot and took a deep breath of damp, earthy air.

"Thirty days," he said softly. "No backing out."

Tercia's eyes glinted. "Thirty days," he agreed. They crawled out into the early light and shook the last bits of dew from their clothes. All around them, the forest floor pulsed with life: writhing roots, curling vines, scuttling insects, each reminding them how small they were—and how large the world they had chosen to conquer could be.

They settled on a flat expanse of ground just beyond their tent, where fallen leaves made a soft carpet. Tercia unfolded a smooth scrap of rock they'd discovered the previous day and set it before them like a canvas. With a piece of charcoal broken from an old campfire stick, Joseph began to sketch a crude map, tracing the broad curve of the nearby stream, marking the fallen log they used as a bench, and outlining the clearing where their shelter stood. Each stroke gave them a feeling of mastery, of turning wild, unknowable space into something they could measure and understand. While Joseph drew, Tercia scribbled notes,

"*Water: safe after boiling,*

Fruit: avoid yellow berries,

Danger: crossing near root maze..."

By the time the sky had brightened to a soft blue, they had a rough plan to guide their every step for the next month.

Next came the gear check. They laid out the contents of their backpacks in the order they might need them: the tarp, rope, headlamp, rusty knife, metal water bottles, their handful of lentils and rice, the two survival books, and a battered sewing kit. Tercia inspected each item like a jeweler examining a gem. He stitched tears in the tarp using a length of vine fiber, doubling his stitches until the fabric felt sturdy. Joseph wrapped the handle of the knife in cloth strips to improve his grip and tested how tight the sheath fit against his belt. They passed the water bottles one by one, pouring out and refilling from the stream, filtering through cloth, then boiling until the water danced with bubbles. While the water heated, they labeled each bottle with a smear of charcoal: 1 through 10 on one, 11 through 20 on the next, and 21 through 30 on the last. It was a small ritual, but it grounded them—turning an abstract notion of time into tangible marks they could track.

By mid-morning, hunger drove them to taste the lentils. They measured exact portions and discussed their foraging plan. Tercia spoke haltingly at first, then gained momentum: mornings for fruit gathering, when the canopy was still quiet; late mornings for water collection; afternoons for traps and fishing. Joseph challenged him: "What if the season changes? What if we can't find fruit that day?" They argued until they arrived at a system of flexibility: follow the schedule when possible, but adapt if circumstances—rain, migrating animals, unexpected safety hazards—forced a change. Each debate, each compromise, made the plan more resilient.

They spent the next hour practicing their traps. They dug a shallow pit, lined it with sticks, and camouflaged the opening with leaves. They fashioned a snare from thin vines and tested its tension around a low branch. The exercises were humbling; nothing worked perfectly the first time. Joseph swore under his breath when the pit collapsed on itself, and Tercia laughed so hard he nearly fell into it. But by the end, they had two functional traps and a makeshift spear that Joseph used to spear a small fish in the shallow pool at the stream's edge. The catch was puny, but when they shared it, each bite tasted of triumph and utter relief.

Their bodies needed conditioning too, so they established a routine of morning stretches and basic calisthenics. They crawled under logs to mimic escaping predators, climbed trees to build upper-body strength, and practiced walking barefoot across rough ground to harden their soles. Every bruise, every cut, was catalogued in their journals—a reminder that their skin, like their resolve, was toughening day by day.

As the sun dipped low, they paused for a moment of ceremony. Joseph gathered a few stones and arranged them in a small circle; inside he placed their map, one water bottle, and the fish they had caught. Around it, they lit a single flame and watched the flickering light dance on the leaves above. Tercia placed his hand on each item. "This flame," he said, voice quiet, "burns for our promise." Joseph nodded, the weight of the next thirty days settling on his shoulders with both fear and exhilaration. With a gentle breath, they snuffed the flame, careful not to waste fuel.

Night fell, and they settled into their shelter, side by side, hearts pounding with anticipation. Each sound in the darkness felt magnified: the drip of water, the snap of a twig, the distant cry of a night bird. But beneath the tension lay something stronger: a shared conviction that whatever the month held, they would face it together. And as they drifted into a restless sleep, the jungle watched over them, alive with possibility.

Chapter 7
The King of the Jungle

Night had just fallen when Joseph woke up. He heard a deep growl in the distance. He quickly woke up Tercia. They lay quietly, scared, listening to the sounds of the dark forest. The fire they had built earlier was now just glowing coals. The only light came from the moon, shining through the trees. The growl came again—it was louder and more powerful this time.

"Jaguar," Tercia whispered with fear. He quietly left the shelter without making a sound. Joseph followed and found Tercia hiding behind a fallen tree, staring into a small clearing. There, standing under the moonlight, was a jaguar. Its spotted fur seemed to glow, and its golden eyes looked wise and powerful.

For a moment, everything went still. The jaguar took a slow step forward. Its muscles moved under its fur. Joseph felt like he couldn't breathe. Tercia held a rusty knife tightly in his hand. They didn't move or make a sound.

The jaguar let out a soft, deep sound. Then it looked straight at Tercia. Time felt like it had stopped. The boys felt tiny and helpless. But the jaguar didn't attack. It just stared at them, like it was trying to understand who they were.

Joseph remembered what Tercia had once said: "Stay calm. Show respect." Slowly, Joseph made himself visible. He bowed his head slightly and opened his hands to show he meant no harm. Tercia did the same.

The jaguar's growl turned into a quiet purr. It sat down calmly, like it was just watching them. Joseph looked at Tercia, who looked scared but amazed at the same time.

After a while, the jaguar stood up and walked closer. It sniffed the air near them and made a soft sound, like a puff of breath. Then it turned and walked away, stopping to look back at them as if to say, "Come with me."

Tercia took a small step forward. Joseph followed him, heart pounding. They stood just behind the jaguar at the edge of the clearing. Under the moonlight, they could see it clearly—strong legs, sharp claws, a long tail moving gently. The jaguar was quiet, powerful, and full of grace. It was the true king of the jungle.

The jaguar slowly disappeared into the trees. When it was gone, Tercia let out a deep breath. "I thought it was going to attack us," he said.

Joseph shook his head. "It respected us because we respected it." He picked up a smooth stone and looked at it. "That's the real king of the jungle—not people. And it taught us something important tonight."

In the silence, both boys felt something change inside them. The jungle was not just a place to survive—it was a place to learn.

Every sound, every movement, every tree had meaning. They walked back to their camp quietly, careful not to step on the fire's ashes.

That night, they didn't sleep deeply. Their dreams were filled with the jaguar's glowing eyes and the sound of its soft purr.

When morning came, the forest looked golden in the sunrise. They felt different—wiser and more thankful.

They decided to leave a bowl of fresh water in the clearing as a thank-you to the jaguar.

From now on, they would act with more respect and care. They weren't just boys trying to survive anymore—they were students of the wild, learning from the true king of the jungle.

Chapter 8
Josia and the Forest Threads

The humid jungle air clung to Tercia's skin as he crouched near the campfire, trying to sharpen a stick. A sudden *rip* startled both boys—Tercia's shirt had snagged on a branch and torn right down the side.

"Great," he muttered, holding up the ripped fabric. "Now I'm half shirtless."

Joseph chuckled. "Well, we're in a jungle. Fashion rules don't apply."

Still, they knew he'd need something to protect him from bugs, sunburn, and the occasional scratch. They sat by their fruit tree camp, thinking. Joseph picked up a bundle of strong vines and started twisting them absently.

"You know," he said, "maybe we can make something. Like a jungle shirt."

Tercia raised an eyebrow. "You want me to wear leaves?"

"No," Joseph said, "not just leaves. Bark, vines, maybe those big banana-like leaves. Something stitched with thorns or plant fiber. You'd be surprised what works when you're desperate."

It took them most of the afternoon. They stripped long leaves, softened bark with water, and wove everything together with twisted vines. It was rough and uneven, but in the end, they created a makeshift tunic. Tercia slipped it on and stood tall.

"Okay," he said, striking a pose, "how do I look?"

"Not bad," Joseph said, giving him a thumbs up. "Jungle couture."

Tercia laughed. For a moment, they both forgot how far they were from home.

But as dusk approached, the forest grew quieter. Too quiet.

Suddenly, there was a familiar sound—the soft crunch of leaves. The boys froze.

They knew that sound.

Golden eyes appeared in the shadows. The jaguar stepped out into the fading light, its muscular form gliding silently across the clearing. But there was no growl this time. No threat. It walked with slow confidence and sat just a few feet away, tail flicking gently.

This time, there was no fear. Tercia knelt and held out a hand. The jaguar sniffed, then gently nudged it with her nose.

"I think it trusts us," Joseph whispered.

"Yeah," Tercia said softly. "We need to give it a name."

Joseph tilted his head. "Like what?"

They both thought for a moment, then Tercia smiled. "Something that includes both of us. Like... Josia."

Joseph blinked. "Jo-seph and Ter-cia... Josia." He nodded. "That's perfect."

They looked at the jaguar again. "Your name is Josia now," Tercia said gently.

The jaguar gave a slow blink and a quiet chuff, almost like approval. Then it lay down near their camp, paws tucked under its chest, tail curled. As if it had always belonged there.

From that evening on, Josia stayed close—watching, listening, even following at a distance during their daily walks. The boys didn't try to tame it. It wasn't a pet. It was something else—wild, majestic, and mysteriously loyal.

Josia became part of their little family. Not through force, but through mutual trust.

And as the fire crackled and night crept in, Tercia scratched at his new leafy shirt and muttered, "I still miss cotton."

Joseph laughed. "You're lucky you even have a shirt."

They both looked over at Josia, who was already dozing under the fruit tree, peaceful and calm.

In that quiet jungle night, three very different creatures—two boys and a jaguar—shared something rare: understanding.

Chapter 9
Facing the Thunderstorm

The air was heavy. Still. The kind of stillness that felt wrong—like the jungle was holding its breath. Joseph noticed it first. Birds that usually chattered from the canopy were silent. Even the insects had gone quiet.

Tercia looked up at the sky, frowning. "Is it just me," he said, "or does the sky look like it's about to explode?"

Joseph followed his gaze. Thick, gray clouds had rolled in from the east, swallowing the blue sky. A low rumble echoed through the jungle. Josia, lying nearby, lifted his head and stared toward the darkening horizon.

"That's not good," Joseph said.

Minutes later, the wind arrived. It didn't whisper—it slammed into the forest, bending branches and sending leaves spiraling through the air. The fruit tree above their camp swayed, and one of their drying cloths blew off the line.

"Get the tarp!" Tercia shouted, running to gather their supplies. They scrambled to secure their small shelter—made of vines, sticks, and a patched-together tarp—and placed rocks on its corners to hold it down.

Thunder cracked so loudly it made Tercia flinch. "That was close!"

Rain followed—first in fat, slow drops, then suddenly in sheets. It fell so hard it was like the sky had cracked open. Their fire hissed and vanished in seconds.

Josia darted into a thicket, seeking shelter under a large overhanging rock. Joseph and Tercia ducked beneath their tarp, knees drawn to their chests, watching the rain flood the jungle floor.

"I've never seen rain like this," Joseph said, his voice barely audible over the storm.

Tercia nodded, water dripping from his hair. "Everything's gonna be soaked. Our food—our stuff..."

Joseph reached into a cloth sack, pulling out a small bundle of wet bananas and smoked fish. "Too late," he said.

The storm raged for what felt like hours. Thunder boomed above them, and flashes of lightning lit the trees in eerie white bursts. Wind tore at their tarp. One corner ripped loose and flapped wildly.

Tercia lunged and grabbed it, his hand slipping on the wet material. "Help me!" he yelled.

Joseph jumped forward and the two of them wrestled with the tarp, retying it with trembling fingers. Every sound felt louder in the storm—every creak of the branches, every gust of wind. For a moment, they felt small and helpless, as if nature itself had turned against them.

But they didn't give up.

They huddled together, covering their supplies with leaves and spare cloth. They used their bodies to shield the few dry items they had left. Outside, Josia's eyes glinted faintly in the dark, unbothered by the chaos. The jaguar seemed to understand: this was the jungle's way of testing them.

Finally, as quickly as it had come, the storm began to slow. The wind died down. The thunder rumbled farther and farther away, and the rain softened to a steady drizzle.

The jungle stirred again. A distant monkey called. A frog croaked. Life resumed.

Joseph crawled out from under the shelter, soaked and shivering. "Well," he said, wringing out his shirt, "we survived that."

Tercia followed, his legs muddy, hair dripping. "Barely."

Josia padded over, shaking rain from his fur. He rubbed his head gently against Joseph's side, then did the same to Tercia. The boys looked at each other, surprised.

"He's proud of us," Tercia said, grinning.

Joseph laughed. "Or he's just wet and wants us to be wet, too."

They started rebuilding their camp as the morning light crept in through the broken clouds. Branches had snapped. Their food was waterlogged. Their tools were scattered.

But they were still standing.

That day, the boys learned something new: **survival wasn't just about being brave—it was about adapting, about holding on when everything feels like it's falling apart.**

And with Josia beside them, they knew they could face even more.

Chapter 10
Josia to the Rescue

It started out like any other day in the jungle.

The sun filtered softly through the trees as Tercia and Joseph trekked deeper into the forest in search of dry wood and fruit. Josia followed a few paces behind, his padded steps silent on the leafy ground.

They had grown more confident—maybe too confident.

"Over there," Tercia called out, spotting a low-hanging bunch of papayas. He climbed a nearby rock and reached for them, steadying himself with one hand. Joseph stepped forward, eyes scanning for danger—just as he always did.

But this time, he missed it.

The rock Tercia stood on crumbled.

It happened fast—his foot slipped, and he tumbled forward. There was a sharp yelp, and then silence. Joseph ran to his side, heart hammering.

Tercia was lying on his side, clutching his leg. Blood was already soaking through his pants where a sharp piece of stone had sliced into his thigh. The gash was deep. Too deep.

Joseph dropped to his knees. "Tercia! Stay with me—don't move!"

Tercia gritted his teeth, his face pale. "I'm fine," he said through clenched jaws, "just... stop the bleeding."

Joseph yanked off his own shirt, tearing it with shaking hands. He wrapped it tightly around the wound, tying it off as best he could. "I don't know if this is enough," he muttered.

Josia stood nearby, tail flicking, ears alert. He stared at Tercia, then at Joseph—then suddenly turned and bounded into the jungle.

"Josia?" Joseph called after him. "Where are you going?"

There was no answer. Only the rustle of leaves as the jaguar vanished.

Tercia lay back against the rock, his breathing shallow. "We need herbs," he said weakly. "The kind we saw near the waterfall. Remember? The healing kind."

Joseph looked toward the dense forest, torn. He couldn't leave Tercia. But Josia had already gone.

"I hope you're right," he whispered. "I hope he remembers."

Minutes crawled by. The jungle pressed in around them—humid, heavy. The cloth around Tercia's leg was soaked through. His skin had gone pale, and his lips trembled.

Then—leaves rustled.

Josia returned.

In his jaws, gently held, was a bundle of long green leaves and a handful of small, red-stemmed herbs. Joseph's eyes widened.

"You... You actually did it?"

The jaguar padded forward and set the bundle down beside Tercia.

Joseph didn't hesitate. He crushed the leaves with a stone, making a pulp, then carefully spread the mixture across the wound. Tercia winced, but said nothing.

Joseph wrapped it again with a cleaner strip of cloth, tying it tight.

An hour passed. Then another. Slowly, Tercia's breathing grew easier. The bleeding had stopped. Color returned to his cheeks.

"You're going to be okay," Joseph said, wiping sweat from his brow.

Tercia gave him a tired smile. "All thanks to Josia."

They both turned to the jaguar, who now lay curled beside them, eyes half-closed, chest rising and falling in a slow rhythm. He looked like he'd done this a hundred times before.

Joseph shook his head in awe. "He's more than a companion now."

"He's our guardian," Tercia said softly. "Our family."

And in the silence that followed, the bond between the three deepened. In a jungle that could so easily take life away, Josia had given it back.

Chapter 11
The Bow, The Hunt, and A Heavy Heart

The sun had just risen, casting golden beams through the trees, when Joseph stood up from the damp earth and wiped the sweat from his brow. "We can't keep living on fruits and roots forever," he muttered, glancing at Tercia, who was sharpening a stick with a jagged stone.

Tercia nodded. "We need real food. Protein."

That morning, the two boys made a decision. With vines, flexible sticks, and sharp-tipped wood, they began crafting simple bows and arrows.

It wasn't easy. The string snapped more than once, and their arrows flew in all the wrong directions during practice.

But after a few frustrating hours—and a lot of laughing at themselves—they had something that worked.

By afternoon, they were ready.

Moving silently through the undergrowth, they spotted a pair of jungle chickens pecking near a patch of shrubs.

Tercia crouched low and held his breath. Joseph nodded, drew back his bow, and released.

The arrow struck true. The bird flailed for a moment, then went still. A second shot from Tercia followed, and soon both chickens were lying lifeless on the forest floor.

They didn't cheer.

Instead, they walked over slowly, kneeling beside the fallen birds. Their eyes met, and neither of them spoke for a long moment.

Tercia finally broke the silence. "We did what we had to."

Joseph nodded, but there was a tightness in his chest. "I know. Still feels… wrong."

Back at their camp, they prepared the chickens carefully. Plucking the feathers was messy, and the smell made their stomachs churn. But hunger pressed hard on them, and by nightfall, the meat was roasting over a small fire, sizzling quietly.

They ate in silence, chewing slowly, thoughtfully. It wasn't celebration—it was necessity.

After their meal, Joseph took a small feather and placed it beside the tree where they had seen the jaguar last.

"Thank you," he whispered, not just to the bird, but to the forest itself.

Tercia looked up at the stars. "We're changing, aren't we?"

Joseph nodded. "Yeah. A lot."

And that night, under the blanket of stars, the forest no longer felt like just a place they were surviving.

It felt like a place they were learning to live in—one choice, one lesson, one step at a time.

Chapter 12
The Unfortunate

The sun was setting behind thick clouds, casting a grayish hue over the dense rainforest. Joseph and Tercia had just finished roasting the last bit of their catch for the day. Josia, their loyal jaguar companion, lay nearby with half-closed eyes, tail gently twitching. Despite their hunger and exhaustion, the air felt peaceful—for now.

But deep in the jungle, peace rarely lasted long.

A low rumble began in the distance, like thunder—but not from the sky. Josia's ears perked up. His body stiffened. Joseph noticed the shift immediately.

"What is it?" he whispered, looking into the trees.

Tercia turned too, standing up slowly. "That's not thunder."

Suddenly, rustling leaves turned to crashing branches. Out of the dense forest emerged a pack of wild animals—coatis, peccaries, and behind them, a lean and vicious ocelot, clearly chasing them or being chased. The stampede was headed straight for the boys' camp.

"Run!" Joseph shouted, grabbing their makeshift bow.

But they were surrounded too quickly. The animals, panicked and wild, charged through. Tercia tripped backward over a root, and Joseph barely had time to pull him up when a loud snarl echoed through the chaos.

Josia had leapt forward.

Fangs bared, claws extended, Josia launched himself between the boys and the stampeding animals. His powerful form collided with the ocelot, throwing it off course. With a ferocious roar, Josia held his ground, swiping and snarling at anything that dared to come near the boys.

For minutes that felt like hours, the jungle was filled with snarls, screeches, and the desperate sounds of survival. Joseph and Tercia crouched behind a tree, helpless, watching the blur of movement as their guardian fought to protect them.

Then everything went still.

The animals fled into the trees, and silence returned. The only sound now was the slow, labored breathing coming from Josia.

"Josia!" Tercia cried out, rushing to his side.

The jaguar lay on his side, his body scratched and bleeding. One eye remained open, watching the boys softly. His breath was heavy and rough, chest rising and falling slowly.

Joseph knelt beside him, tears forming. "No... you're okay, right? You'll be okay?"

Tercia stroked Josia's head gently. "You saved us... again."

Despite the pain, Josia gave a soft chuff, his version of a purr, and nudged Tercia's hand with his nose. His strength was fading, but the bond between the three was stronger than ever.

"We need to help him," Joseph said quickly. "We can't let him die."

They worked through the night. Tercia tore strips of cloth from their bags, pressing them gently against the wounds to stop the bleeding. Joseph gathered water and herbs they had seen Josia use before—just in case.

They didn't sleep. They didn't speak much. Their focus was Josia—still, brave Josia.

By dawn, Josia was still alive, but barely. His body was warm but weak. The boys had done all they could. Now, all they could do was wait.

"He saved us, Joseph," Tercia whispered, voice cracking. "He took on everything. For us."

Joseph nodded, eyes fixed on the jaguar's side as it rose and fell. "He's not just a jaguar anymore. He's family."

They stayed beside Josia for the rest of the day, gently caring for him, whispering words of comfort. They didn't know if he'd make it. But they promised each other, no matter what—Josia would never be alone.

Chapter 13
The Shifting

The morning sun filtered through the dense canopy, casting golden beams onto the forest floor. Josia, now fully recovered and more majestic than ever, stretched beside the boys' camp. It had been a calm few days, but water was becoming harder to find, and their shelter was slowly wearing out. It was time for a change.

Joseph swung himself onto Josia's broad back. The jaguar was strong and graceful, gliding through the jungle like a shadow. From atop his furry companion, Joseph had a better view of the land. They passed towering trees, thick vines, and even crossed a muddy patch where frogs leapt in every direction. The jungle was teeming with life, but Joseph was searching for something more—a place where they could thrive.

Every few minutes, Joseph would make a mental note of the land—how flat it was, whether there were signs of nearby predators, and the presence of birds or small animals that might indicate fresh water. After nearly an hour of riding, Joseph spotted it: a gentle slope leading to a crystal-clear spring. The water sparkled under the sun, and wild fruits grew nearby—bananas, papayas, and even guavas. The land around the spring was flat and shaded, perfect for building a new shelter. Joseph's heart soared. He had found it.

Excited and unable to contain his discovery, Joseph leaned forward and whispered, "Let's go back." Josia responded with a quiet chuff, turning around and racing through the underbrush with confidence and speed.

He returned to camp brimming with excitement. "Tercia! I found it!" he shouted, jumping off Josia. Tercia, who had been sorting firewood, looked up with wide eyes. "Really?"

Joseph nodded. "Fresh water, fruits, space for shelter—it's all there."

Before they left, Josia surprised them again. Using a thick, curved stone he had dragged in his mouth and a strong vine, he had managed to help them craft a crude axe. Joseph and Tercia added a wooden handle to it, binding it tight. With the axe, chopping thick sticks and clearing land became ten times easier.

They began gathering their materials for the big move. Josia carried a small bundle on his back while Joseph and Tercia packed everything into large palm-leaf sacks. It was a long journey, but spirits were high. When they arrived, the sound of the spring was music to their ears. They dropped everything and drank deeply from the cool, clear water.

They immediately began working on the shelter. The axe cut through wood easily, and Josia helped drag logs into place. They used vines as rope and layered leaves to make a waterproof roof. It was slow, sweaty work, but incredibly satisfying.

By evening, the shelter was half-built. They had also set up a cooking area, a place to store dry food, and even a small corner just for Josia to rest. The boys gathered firewood and roasted some of the guavas they had picked. The sugary scent filled the air, mingling with the earthy aroma of fresh leaves and damp soil.

As they sat by the fire that night, their muscles aching but their hearts full, Tercia said, "This place feels like it chose us."

Joseph nodded, looking up at the moonlight streaming through the trees. "It's perfect. We can do anything here."

Josia, lying nearby with his head resting on his paws, gave a soft purr in agreement. They weren't just building a new camp—they were building a life.

Over the next few days, they refined the shelter, built a makeshift fence to keep wild animals away, and organized their supplies better than ever before. They even carved symbols into the bark of trees to mark paths and create a map of their surroundings.

They tested the spring water for freshness each morning, found new edible plants nearby, and collected stones to make tools. The forest seemed to welcome them more with each passing day.

At one point, they found a fallen tree trunk hollowed out inside. Joseph turned it into a bench, while Tercia stacked smooth stones to build a tiny stove-like fire pit. They added a drying area to preserve fruits, a simple rack made of sticks and vines.

Every part of their new life was crafted with care, patience, and pride. They no longer felt like two lost orphans in a jungle—they felt like a team, supported by Josia and guided by instinct and experience.

This wasn't just a shift in location. It was a shift in their journey. A chapter that started with searching ended in discovery, and the jungle no longer felt like a stranger. It was home.

Chapter 14
A Strange New Friend

The sun had barely reached its peak when Joseph and Tercia decided it was finally time to build something bigger. Their new location was perfect in every way—abundant water, fresh fruits, sturdy shelter—but they needed more space. The rains had been unpredictable lately, and if they wanted to survive a full month here, they would need a large tent for extra protection.

With Josia's help, they began tying thick leaves to long, solid sticks. It was a challenging task, especially since the tent had to be large enough to store food, tools, and even act as a second sleeping area during heavy rain. The boys worked tirelessly, tying knots with vines and hammering stakes into the soft ground with rocks.

While they were laying the final structure, Josia's ears suddenly twitched. The jaguar stood still, nose in the air, sniffing. Then came a low growl—not threatening, but curious. Joseph looked up. "What is it, girl?"

Out of the dense underbrush came a small creature, no bigger than a housecat, yet something about it felt... off. Its fur was patterned in a way neither of them had ever seen—short like a dog's, but with stripes like a wild cat. It had the sharp, alert eyes of a feline but the floppy ears and happy tail of a pup. The creature stared at them, unmoving.

Tercia stepped back. "What is that? Is it... a dog?"

Joseph blinked. "Or a cat?"

Josia made a soft chuff and approached the creature slowly. To their amazement, the hybrid didn't run. Instead, it wagged its tail and purred—at the same time. Tercia let out a laugh. "Okay, that's definitely not something we've ever seen before."

They knelt and observed it. The animal had strong limbs, padded feet perfect for climbing, and sharp teeth that peeked from its friendly mouth. It rubbed itself against Josia's leg, and the big jaguar didn't seem to mind. In fact, she gave a low rumble of approval.

"Looks like she likes it," Joseph said, smiling.

They named the creature "Toseph"—from "T" from Tercia and "oseph,"from Joseph. Over the next few hours, Toseph became part of the group, following Josia and even helping Joseph and Tercia fetch vines. Its sense of smell was remarkable, leading them to a new stash of wild berries nearby.

That evening, as the tent finally took shape, the boys sat with their two companions around the fire.

Tercia leaned back and stared at the stars. "We didn't just find a home," he whispered. "We found a family."

Josia rested beside him, and Toseph curled into a ball near the fire. Joseph smiled.

The jungle, once terrifying, was now full of wonder.

With Josia and Toseph by their side, they knew they could face anything.

Their journey wasn't just about surviving anymore—it was about discovering the incredible secrets of the wild and bonding with those they never imagined meeting.

Chapter 15
Echoes of the Past

The sun had just started to warm the jungle floor when Joseph and Tercia decided to explore the area near the river. It was a lazy morning, and they had some free time after tending to their small carrot farm and checking on their fruit supplies. Josia padded alongside them, and their new companion, Toseph, pranced ahead, ears perked and tail wagging.

As they followed the winding path to the river, they stumbled upon something unusual—a pile of giant rocks nestled near the riverbank. But what caught their attention wasn't just the size of the stones. Near one of the boulders, half-buried in the mud, was something metal.

Joseph knelt down and began to clear the dirt away. "It's a box!" he exclaimed. After a few minutes of digging, they managed to lift out a rusted metal container with strange carvings on its lid.

Tercia brushed away the dirt and read the faded letters. "'1883'... This must be more than a hundred years old!" Carefully, they opened it. Inside were photographs, letters, an old compass, a wooden whistle, and a small cloth journal written in old handwriting. They had discovered a time capsule from the 1880s.

"This is... amazing," Tercia whispered, flipping through the journal. "Look at this—maps, notes, even a sketch of the river!"

Joseph held the compass, still surprisingly intact. "We need to keep this safe. It's a piece of history."

They returned to camp and stored the capsule in a wooden chest they had carved out earlier for special collectibles. Tercia, inspired by the discovery, began to craft something new—a tool that could help them further explore the rocky river terrain.

Using wood, sharpened stone, and vines, he made a crude yet sturdy pickaxe. It took the better part of a day, but when he finished, they headed back to the river to put it to the test.

The pickaxe held strong as Tercia swung it against the giant rocks. After several hard strikes, one of the rocks cracked, revealing something unusual inside. Joseph reached in and pulled out a solid, greyish-brown object with a strange spiral shape.

"Wait," Tercia said, examining it closely. "That's not just a rock. That's a fossil!"

It looked like a preserved shell from an ancient marine creature, perfectly embedded in the stone. Their eyes widened with wonder.

They had found something incredible—proof that the area they were in might have been underwater millions of years ago.

That night, they sat around the fire, the fossil resting between them, the time capsule safely stored beside their tent. Toseph rested with his head on Josia's back, and the firelight danced across their faces.

"Today felt like magic," Joseph said quietly.

Tercia nodded. "It's like the jungle is slowly sharing its secrets with us."

Josia let out a low purr and looked toward the trees, calm and alert as always. Even in this wild place, with its dangers and unknowns, moments like these made it feel like home.

Later that night, Tercia re-read the notes in the journal they'd found. It spoke of explorers, early settlers, and curious scientists who tried to understand the mysteries of the Amazon. "They were like us," he whispered. "Trying to learn, trying to survive."

Joseph smiled. "And now it's our turn to leave something behind."

The next day, they built a wooden shelf just for their collectibles—fossils, old tools, rare plants, and now the 1880s time capsule. They decided they'd add one object from each discovery they made.

For the first time since arriving in the jungle, they felt like they were building something lasting—something that could maybe help someone in the future, just like the explorers from the past helped them now.

Their jungle adventure was no longer just about survival. It was about discovery. About learning. About listening to what the forest wanted to tell them.

Chapter 16
The Farmers of the Amazon

After days of surviving on fruits, the occasional animal, and foraged roots, Joseph and Tercia began thinking more seriously about long-term food. They had already faced storms, wild animals, and hunger. If they were going to stay for a month, they needed more than luck and good instincts—they needed a plan.

One morning, Joseph woke up unusually early, stirred by the soft rustling of the jungle and the scent of wet earth after a light rain. Josia and Toseph were asleep nearby, curled beside the fire pit. Tercia was still snoring lightly. Joseph stepped out quietly, picking up a small wooden spade they had carved earlier, and wandered toward the patch of land they'd noticed on a previous exploration.

It was a small clearing, sunlight pouring in from above where the trees had thinned. The ground was soft, dark, and smelled rich—like the kind of soil they had only read about in school science books. Joseph knelt and dug a handful of earth. It was loose, full of nutrients and decaying leaves. He grinned. This was it. The perfect place to start a farm.

Later that morning, he brought Tercia and the animals to see the spot. "If we grow our own food here," Joseph said, "we don't have to hunt as often. And carrots are supposed to grow well in this kind of soil."

Tercia nodded. "We've got seeds from the few we collected back at the orphanage. Remember those packets in our survival pouch? I never thought we'd actually use them."

The next few days were filled with effort. They cleared the land using their handmade axe, Josia even helping by dragging away large branches. Toseph, always curious, kept digging shallow holes with his paws and nose, often where they didn't want him to. But the boys didn't mind. Their little team felt more like a family than ever.

They tilled the soil with sharpened sticks, laid out rows with stones, and finally, one by one, planted the carrot seeds. They watered them from their nearby stream and checked on them every morning. Though they knew it would take time for anything to grow, the act of planting brought them peace. They were no longer just surviving; they were building something that could sustain them.

After a week, tiny green sprouts peeked out from the soil. Tercia was the first to spot them and jumped with excitement. "Look!" he shouted. "We did it! They're growing!"

It was a small victory, but to them, it felt like they'd discovered treasure. Every day they watched the sprouts grow taller. They started calling their plot "The Farm," even though it was just a few rows of carrots in the jungle.

To protect the plants from being trampled, they built a simple fence from sticks and vines. Josia patrolled the area during the night, while Toseph stayed close, occasionally chasing off curious birds.

Joseph began carving signs out of bark, labeling different rows. "Next time," he told Tercia, "we'll try tomatoes or maybe beans."

Tercia laughed. "Let's just get through the carrots first."

In the evenings, they sat around their fire, talking about what they would do if the carrots actually grew large and edible. Would they boil them? Roast them over the fire? Could they even mash them and try to bake something? The conversations made them feel closer—like they weren't just lost kids in the middle of nowhere, but explorers, creators, and thinkers.

By now, they had settled into a routine. They'd farm in the morning, explore or repair their shelter in the afternoon, and read old pages from their journal by the fire. Josia had become more than a wild animal—he was family. Toseph, too, was a constant joy, always finding ways to make them laugh even on the hardest days.

A few days later, while gathering water, Joseph noticed how strong the carrot tops had become. He tugged gently at one, and to his shock, a small, orange root came out. "Tercia!" he called. "They're ready!"

Together, they harvested their first batch—only five carrots, but each one felt like a trophy. They roasted them slowly, savoring the taste more than anything they'd eaten since arriving. The carrots were warm, a little sweet, and slightly crunchy. They weren't perfect, but they were theirs.

That night, as they sat by the fire with Josia and Toseph lying beside them, Joseph leaned back and looked up at the stars.

"We're not just surviving anymore," he said. "We're living."

Tercia nodded, resting his hands behind his head. "And we're learning what it means to build a life—even in the middle of nowhere."

The jungle was still wild and unpredictable, but for now, they had food, fire, friendship, and a bit of hope. And for two boys who had once been just orphans,

Chapter 17
Toseph Finds Something Bony

The jungle was quiet that morning, too quiet. Even the birdsong seemed softer, as if the forest was holding its breath. Joseph and Tercia were tending to their carrot patch, checking for weeds and watering the soil. Josia lay stretched out under the shade of a large fern, eyes half-closed. Toseph, however, had disappeared.

At first, they didn't think much of it. Toseph often wandered off on his own adventures—chasing butterflies, investigating new smells, or digging up bugs. But when an hour passed and he still hadn't returned, Joseph started getting worried.

"Toseph!" he called out into the trees. "Toseph, where are you, buddy?"

No reply.

Josia immediately stood and sniffed the air, ears alert. Tercia grabbed his handmade spear. "We should look for him," he said, trying to keep calm. "He might've gotten stuck or... hurt."

Following Josia's lead, they began to trek through the undergrowth, weaving between vines and ducking under low branches. Eventually, Josia came to a stop and let out a low, questioning growl. Just ahead, partially hidden by moss and vines, was a dark opening in a cliffside.

"A cave," Joseph muttered. "No wonder we've never seen this before."

From inside, they heard a soft, frightened whimper. "That's him!" Tercia exclaimed. Without a second thought, the two boys entered the cave, Josia close behind.

Inside, the air was cold and musty. It smelled like stone, dampness, and something... older. The cave walls were rough and jagged, and the light from the outside quickly faded. Joseph lit a small torch they had made earlier that week, and its glow flickered across the rock surfaces.

Then they saw Toseph.

He was crouched near a wall, tail between his legs, ears flat, staring at something with wide, frightened eyes. When they reached him, he didn't move. He just kept staring ahead—at a skeleton.

It lay slumped against the cave wall, partially covered in dust and vines. The bones were yellowed with age, and some were scattered, but the skull was still intact, its empty eye sockets staring into the darkness. Bits of torn fabric clung to the ribcage, and an old leather boot lay nearby.

Tercia gasped. "A person... someone really died here."

They stood in silence for a moment, the torch casting eerie shadows on the walls. Toseph let out a low whimper and pressed himself against Joseph's leg.

Joseph bent down and gently patted Toseph's head. "It's okay. You did good, buddy. You found something important."

Tercia leaned closer to inspect the skeleton. "Who could this have been? A traveler? An explorer? Maybe someone like us who got lost?"

They searched the cave carefully. Nearby, they found an old backpack, mostly rotted, but inside was a small journal—its pages damp but still readable. Tercia opened it carefully.

"There's a name inside. 'Eduardo M.' And a date... 1912." He flipped through more pages. "It's written in Portuguese. He must've been an explorer."

As they read, the pieces slowly came together. Eduardo had ventured deep into the jungle, mapping uncharted territory. But something had gone wrong. He mentioned getting injured and hiding in a cave to rest. The last entry was shaky, the ink faded. It read: *If I do not survive, may this place remember me.*

Joseph's voice was quiet. "He never made it out."

Tercia nodded, still staring at the skeleton. "We should do something."

They agreed to bury the bones just outside the cave and mark the spot with stones. It felt right. Eduardo had died alone, but now he wouldn't be forgotten. They built a small cross from branches and carved his initials into a stone at the base. Toseph sat silently beside them the whole time.

After the burial, the boys took one final look into the cave, now strangely less frightening. They decided to clean it up and store the journal with their other discoveries back at camp. The cave would be a place of respect—Eduardo's resting place.

As the sun began to set, the group made their way back to their clearing. Toseph stayed close to Joseph, no longer playful, but quiet and thoughtful. Even Josia walked more slowly than usual, as if the jungle itself had been reminded of something solemn.

That night, around the fire, they added Eduardo's journal to their wooden chest. Joseph whispered a soft thank you to the explorer who had once walked the same forest paths.

And though they would continue their journey the next day, they knew one thing for certain—this forest had many secrets, and each one changed them just a little more.

Chapter 18
The Crash

It was a quiet morning after the burial of Eduardo. The forest had taken on a stillness that even the wind seemed to respect. The boys hadn't spoken much since the discovery of the skeleton and journal. Toseph was still cautious, always glancing behind bushes, and Josia seemed unusually alert, sniffing the air more often than usual.

Joseph and Tercia were walking deeper into the jungle that day—not for food or water, but simply to clear their minds. The jungle, unpredictable as ever, had become something of a teacher. Every day it revealed new lessons: about patience, respect, survival, and now—history.

Just twenty minutes into their walk, Joseph stopped in his tracks. "What is that?" he said, pointing at something gleaming behind a wall of thick vines.

Tercia stepped forward, pushing aside the greenery. His breath caught in his throat. "No way..."

Before them, partially buried in the earth and wrapped in thick moss, was a twisted piece of metal—shiny, silver, and unnaturally smooth. It had markings. English letters, faded but still readable.

They both stood frozen. It was a **piece of an airplane**.

Josia padded forward, sniffing it cautiously, while Toseph circled around the side. The metal was broken and rusted at the edges.

A large section of the plane's side was intact, with a torn seatbelt hanging from what was once a row of seats. The broken skeleton of a window was cracked but still gave a clear view inside.

Tercia stepped closer and ran his fingers across the jagged lettering on the side. "P-A-C—Pacific Airways," he read aloud. "That's an airline... but from when?"

They climbed over the edge, finding bits of luggage, wires, metal scraps, and torn cloth. Joseph pulled out a rusted nameplate bolted to the side.

"Flight 09-B. 1912," he read.

The same year as Eduardo's last journal entry.

They looked at each other, the connection forming silently between them.

"You think... Eduardo was on this plane?" Tercia asked quietly.

Joseph nodded slowly. "Maybe he survived the crash. Maybe that's how he ended up here."

They searched the wreck for clues. Among the rubble, they found a logbook—half-burnt and sealed in a tin case. The ink had smudged from moisture, but a few entries were readable. It spoke of engine failure mid-flight, poor visibility, and an emergency landing attempt deep in the rainforest. The last entry confirmed what they feared: the plane had gone down hard. No exact coordinates, no rescue. Just silence after impact.

They sat for a moment in the shadow of the wreckage. It was strange how the jungle had taken over the place. Vines snaked through the metal frame, and birds nested in old seat cushions. It was no longer just a crash site—it was part of the forest now.

Tercia wiped his forehead, his hand shaking slightly. "It's weird. I feel like we're walking through someone's last memory."

Joseph nodded, placing the logbook carefully in his bag. "Let's bring this back. It belongs with Eduardo's journal."

As they turned to leave, Toseph barked twice, as if calling them to look one more time. On a tree nearby, half-covered in moss, were initials—**E.M.**

Carved roughly with something sharp, probably a knife.

"Eduardo M." Joseph whispered.

"He must've wandered from here," Tercia said, his voice soft. "Injured. Alone. Maybe he was the only one who survived."

Josia let out a low, sorrowful purr. Even he seemed to understand the gravity of the moment.

When they returned to camp, they placed the logbook beside Eduardo's journal. Their little chest of discoveries was becoming more than just a box of objects—it was turning into a museum of forgotten lives, pieced together by two boys and their animal companions.

That night, as the fire crackled, Joseph stared into the flames. "We're not just survivors anymore, Tercia. We're part of something bigger. Like... we were meant to be here."

Tercia nodded slowly, still staring at the logbook. "Eduardo tried to survive just like us. But he didn't have Josia... or Toseph... or anyone."

There was silence for a moment. Then Joseph added, "That's why we'll remember him. So he won't be alone again."

They slept that night with a new sense of responsibility. The jungle wasn't just wild anymore. It was filled with stories. And now, they were the ones who carried them forward.

Chapter 19
Eduardo's Hidden Note

The day after discovering the airplane wreck, Joseph and Tercia were still thinking about the initials carved into the tree. There was something haunting and powerful about Eduardo's presence—even decades later, he was still guiding them.

That morning, while checking through the logbook and the items they had gathered from the crash site, Tercia decided to open the jacket they had brought back with Eduardo's belongings. The fabric was old and stiff, but mostly intact. As he inspected the inside lining, something crinkled beneath the seam. Curious, he reached in and pulled out a folded piece of paper tucked deep inside a hidden pocket.

"Joseph," Tercia said quietly, "I think I found something."

Joseph rushed over. The paper was yellowed and fragile. Tercia carefully unfolded it and laid it flat on a wooden slab they used as a table.

It was a handwritten note.

"To whomever finds this,

I am Eduardo M. This note is not for just anyone. If you are not of my family, I beg you—leave it where it belongs. In the event of my death, please return this to my descendants. Hidden beneath the 'stone eagle' west of this camp lies a metal box. It contains a treasure passed down by generations before me. It is meant only for the blood of the Martins family. Please respect this wish. I die not for gold, but for legacy.

Eduardo M."

For a long while, the jungle around them seemed to disappear. The only thing they could hear was the thudding of their own hearts.

"A treasure?" Joseph whispered.

Tercia looked stunned. "And he left instructions for how to find it..."

The boys read the note again. West of this camp. Stone eagle. A metal box. Eduardo hadn't just been a stranded explorer—he had been a guardian of something ancient, something he considered sacred.

By the time the sun began to lower, they had already searched through maps they'd drawn of the area and marked possible rock formations. With Josia and Toseph by their side, they headed west. After nearly an hour of hiking, they spotted it—what looked like a massive boulder shaped like a bird with wings partially spread.

"The stone eagle," Joseph whispered. "It's real."

They began to dig at the base, pushing aside ferns, soil, and stones. After some time, the sound of metal clinked against Joseph's shovel.

They looked at each other.

Buried beneath was a medium-sized box, rusted and worn but still intact. Carefully, they lifted it from the earth and opened it.

Inside, wrapped in old cloth, were gold coins, an antique compass, a pendant shaped like a lion, and a leather-bound notebook filled with diagrams, old maps, and a letter of inheritance signed by Eduardo himself. There was also a photograph—faded, but still clear—of Eduardo standing with a woman and two young children.

Tercia let out a long breath. "It's real... all of it."

For a long moment, no one spoke.

Back at the camp that night, the treasure lay in front of them, glinting in the firelight. Josia rested nearby, watching them with those knowing, golden eyes. Toseph was curled up against Joseph's feet, snoring softly.

Tercia finally broke the silence. "So... what now?"

Joseph didn't answer right away. He looked at the pendant, then at the picture. "We're not family," he said. "But we found it. Doesn't that mean something?"

Tercia nodded slowly. "Yeah. But Eduardo asked us to return it to his family. What if they're still out there? Maybe they've been searching for this for generations."

"But what if they're gone?" Joseph said. "What if no one's left to give it to? We could use it, Tercia. We've been starving, living off the jungle. This could buy us safety, even change our lives."

Tercia stared into the fire. "Or it could change us."

The silence that followed was deep. Neither boy wanted to say it aloud, but they both felt the same thing: the treasure was tempting. More than anything they'd ever held in their hands. But so was Eduardo's dying wish.

Morning came slowly as if the sun itself was unsure whether to rise. Joseph woke up staring at the treasure box still sitting at the center of their shelter. The gold and heirlooms glinted in the soft light, no less magical than the moment they had discovered it.

Tercia sat cross-legged by the fire, already awake, flipping through Eduardo's leather-bound notebook. Josia and Toseph lay quietly, as if sensing that this was no ordinary morning.

Joseph sat up and broke the silence. "We need to talk."

Tercia looked up. He nodded.

For the next hour, they debated.

"We found it," Joseph said. "We risked our lives in this jungle, got attacked, starved, and fought wild animals. Doesn't that count for something?"

"It does," Tercia replied calmly. "But Eduardo was clear. This was for his family. We aren't that."

"But how do we even find his family?" Joseph pressed. "We don't know where they live, or if they even exist. What if it's lost forever in some museum, or stolen by someone else?"

Tercia hesitated. "What if we're the reason it's remembered properly? What if we're the ones who make sure it gets back where it belongs?"

The silence between them grew thicker.

They both knew the value of what they'd found—enough to possibly change their lives forever. A way out. A reward for surviving the impossible.

But they also knew what Eduardo's note said. *"I die not for gold, but for legacy."*

Eventually, Tercia closed the notebook. "Let's decide when we get out of here."

Joseph exhaled deeply. "Yeah... okay. We don't even know if we'll make it out."

"Then that's our first goal," Tercia said. "Survive. Then we can make the right choice."

They shook hands over the treasure chest—not in greed, but in agreement. For now, it would stay hidden, packed and buried safely until their journey was over.

That afternoon, they decided to explore the cave once more—Eduardo's resting place, where it had all begun. Something kept pulling them back to it, as if the jungle still had one more secret to reveal.

With Josia leading, and Toseph bounding beside them, they returned to the moss-covered entrance. The torchlight flickered off the stone walls as they moved deeper inside. It was colder than before, but they pushed on, climbing over jagged rocks and past the place where Eduardo's remains had once rested.

As they neared the far end of the cave, Toseph suddenly stopped. His ears perked. He sniffed at a pile of loose rocks and barked.

"What is it?" Tercia asked, moving closer.

They dug carefully, removing rocks and pushing aside an old root. And there—buried beneath—was a long, narrow object wrapped in faded cloth.

Joseph unwrapped it slowly, and both boys gasped.

It was a **sword**.

Ancient but beautifully preserved. Its blade was slightly rusted at the edge, but the handle was carved with careful detail—elegant scrollwork and initials engraved into the hilt: **"J.M."**

Attached to it was a tag. The ink was faint, but readable.

"This sword belonged to my grandfather. If you ever find this, please return it to my family. It is part of our bloodline, our story."
- Eduardo M.

The boys were silent.

"It's not just gold," Joseph murmured. "This... this is family history."

Tercia's voice was soft. "Now we have to return it. Somehow, some way."
"Yeah," Joseph said. "But we'll need to get out of the jungle first. Alive."

They wrapped the sword gently and packed it with care. It no longer felt like treasure—it felt like responsibility.

The sun had barely climbed over the canopy when Joseph knelt by the stream, sharpening the blade of a new creation. Josia sat beside him, watching calmly, while Toseph chased butterflies nearby. The forest had become quieter these past few days—as if waiting.

Tercia approached, holding the polished wooden handle they had carved from a thick branch the day before. "Think this will work?" he asked, handing it over.

Joseph took it and slid the newly sharpened metal blade into the carved slot. "Only one way to find out," he replied, tightening it with vines they had soaked and twisted to act like rope.

It had taken them days to perfect. The axe was rough, a mix of iron scraps, jungle wood, and a bit of luck—but it felt solid in Joseph's grip.

They called it **The Sharp Forest-Made Axe**.

"Let's test it," Tercia said, already leading the way toward a thick, aged tree at the edge of their territory. Its bark was hard, its trunk wide. A perfect test.

With one swing, the axe bit deep. Not perfectly clean, but effective. Joseph stepped back, swung again, and this time bark split off in chunks. Tercia grinned. "It works!"

An hour later, the tree gave a long, echoing creak before falling with a deep thud onto the earth, sending birds scattering from the trees above. As the dust settled, Tercia walked to the base where the roots had once held firm—and then froze.

"Joseph..." he whispered. "Come look at this."

Where the tree had stood, its roots had been tangled around a **small stone slab**, flat and partially buried. Tercia brushed away the dirt and vines. Strange markings covered its surface—lines, dots, and what looked like waves.

"Is this... a drawing?" Joseph asked.

The slab was rectangular, and carved into its face was a **crude map**. A coastline. A long river. Several mountain peaks etched into the stone. But what stunned them most was the single word scratched at the bottom, just beneath a small compass rose.

"Almada — Portugal"

They both stared in silence.

"This is... where Eduardo's family is from?" Tercia whispered.

Joseph nodded slowly. "He must've marked the path. This must be the original map he followed—or someone before him."

They gently lifted the slab out from the roots and carried it back to camp. Using charcoal, they copied the design into their journal in case the original got damaged.

The map seemed to tell a story. Starting from Almada, a path was marked across a sea—clearly the Atlantic—then snaking into the jungle, crossing rivers, valleys, and stopping at a circled area. Their current location was nearly identical to that final spot.

"Eduardo or his family must've brought this here... to protect the treasure," Joseph said, pointing. "He was carrying legacy. Not just coins or gold—but something passed down for generations."

Tercia added, "It's all connected. The sword, the box, the map—it all starts in Almada."

They sat in silence, overwhelmed. The treasure, now more than ever, felt sacred. It wasn't about riches anymore. It was about completing something someone else had started—something left unfinished for nearly a century.

The morning was quiet, filled with the soft hum of the jungle. Joseph and Tercia were bent over their small carrot patch, carefully pulling weeds and loosening the soil with their makeshift tools. Josia sat nearby, his golden eyes following every motion, while Toseph darted around playfully, occasionally trying to bite at falling leaves as if they were prey.

The harvest was finally paying off. Carrots were sprouting, and the soil here seemed perfect for crops. They had worked tirelessly to make this little farm, and now it was giving them both food and pride. But that morning, as Joseph pushed his tool deep into the ground, it hit something that sounded different—*a hollow thud.*

"Did you hear that?" Joseph asked, frowning.

Tercia nodded, curiosity lighting his face. "That's not rock. Dig deeper."

They dug side by side, the earth giving way until a flat, metallic surface appeared beneath the roots of their crops. They exchanged nervous looks.

"It's... a hatch," Joseph whispered. His hands brushed dirt away to reveal a rusted handle, almost invisible under layers of soil.

With effort, they pulled it open. The old hatch creaked loudly, sending a shiver through the air, as if it had been sealed for centuries. A cool gust of stale air rose up from below.

"What is this place?" Tercia muttered, peering into the darkness.

Holding torches made of sticks and sap, they descended a narrow ladder into the hidden underground space. The deeper they went, the more the smell of age and dust filled their lungs.

The bunker beneath their camp was larger than they expected—stone walls lined with carvings, and the ground littered with bones. At first, they thought they had stumbled upon a graveyard, but as Joseph raised his torch higher, they realized the truth.

Dozens of **skulls** lined the shelves carved into the walls. Each skull had been arranged neatly, almost like trophies.

Tercia's breath caught. "This... this was a war bunker. These skulls... they mark victories. Amazon tribes fought here."

Joseph shuddered. "It feels like their ghosts are still watching us."

Josia growled lowly, his fur standing on end. Toseph pressed closer to Tercia, whining.

As they explored further, Joseph's torch flickered against something odd—a small box tucked into a corner, half-buried under dirt and bones. He pulled it free and slowly opened it.

Inside lay **six or seven gold coins**, their surfaces glinting in the firelight despite the years. Alongside them was a folded, yellowed piece of paper.

Tercia read it aloud, his voice echoing in the bunker:

"To the finder—these coins belong to you. Whoever uncovers this place, let it be known: these treasures are yours to keep. I, Eduardo, discovered this bunker long ago, but I chose not to

take more than what I could carry. This land belongs to the Amazons, but these coins are a gift from me... to you."

The two brothers stood frozen.

"Eduardo was here," Joseph whispered. "Right here, where we're standing."

Tercia clutched the letter, his hands trembling. "He must have uncovered this long before us. And he left these coins... waiting for someone to find them."

They carefully carried the coins and the letter back to their camp. The bunker below still lingered in their minds—dark, heavy with history, filled with skulls that told of bloody wars. Yet, amidst the shadows, Eduardo's gift felt like a strange spark of hope.

That night, as the coins shimmered faintly in the firelight, Joseph spoke quietly: "Every discovery pulls us closer to Eduardo's past... and to the truth about why we're here."

Tercia nodded, staring at the gold. "But it also makes the choices harder. Do we keep these? Or do we return them too, with everything else?"

"Do you think we'll ever get there?" Tercia asked, glancing at the map.

"I don't know," Joseph said. "But if we ever do make it out of here, we know where to go."

"We'll return the sword," Tercia said quietly. "And the box."

Joseph nodded. "Even if it takes years."

The jungle hummed around them, but inside the camp, everything felt clearer. They had uncovered more than a treasure. They had found a purpose.

A reason to keep going.

And the journey, it seemed, was just beginning.

Chapter 20
The Wolf Warning

It was just past midnight when a chill crept through the jungle. The fire had burned low, casting flickers of light on the surrounding trees. Joseph and Tercia lay asleep inside their shelter, curled up in their hammocks, while Josia kept watch nearby, ears perked, and body still.

Toseph stirred restlessly, then let out a quiet growl.

Josia stood up, alert.

A soft rustling came from the brush behind them—too soft for wind, too steady for leaves. Josia let out a low warning growl. The sound was enough to jolt Tercia awake.

"What is it?" he whispered, sitting up.

Before anyone could answer, a deep snarl tore through the quiet. Two glowing eyes appeared in the darkness. Then another. Then a third.

"Joseph, wake up!" Tercia hissed.

Joseph bolted upright just in time to see the **first wolf** emerge from the undergrowth, teeth bared, fur matted with dirt and leaves. Its eyes were wild. And it wasn't alone. Three more figures followed—silent, purposeful.

They weren't the confused or frightened animals the boys had encountered before. These were **predators**, and they were hunting.

Josia leapt in front of the boys, his shoulders squared and his fangs bared. A snarl rippled through his throat as he crouched low, ready to attack.

Then came a blur—**Toseph**, eyes blazing, shot forward and lunged at the nearest wolf, clamping his jaws around its foreleg. A sickening crunch followed. The wolf howled in pain and scrambled back, dragging its wounded leg behind it.

The others hesitated, circling. One lunged toward Joseph, but Josia met it mid-air, throwing it to the ground in a tangle of fur and claws. The scuffle was violent and quick—Josia's strength won out.

The wolves regrouped, growling in low, eerie unison.

Then, something unexpected happened.

One of them, taller than the rest with a ragged scar across its muzzle, stepped forward—not to attack, but to stare. Its yellow eyes locked onto the boys. It didn't move. It didn't snarl. It just... looked.

And then it growled—not angrily, but deeply, like thunder rumbling in a distant sky.

Tercia felt something cold run through his veins. "Joseph," he whispered, "It's warning us."

Joseph's eyes didn't leave the wolf. "This wasn't a random attack," he said slowly. "They know we're here."

"They'll come back," Joseph agreed. "That growl... it wasn't over. It was just beginning."

The lead wolf let out a final snarl, then turned and disappeared into the jungle. The others followed, silent shadows fading into the night.

The jungle was still dripping from the previous night's storm. Joseph and Tercia pushed forward slowly, following the river's edge. The mud clung to their boots, and the air was heavy with dampness, yet hope carried them forward—just a mile more, and they would finally leave the endless green behind.

But the Amazon never let anyone leave so easily.

A low growl cut through the air. Joseph froze, his hand tightening around the stick he had given Tercia. His eyes scanned the shadows between the trees. Then he saw them. Yellow eyes glowed from the undergrowth—one pair, then another, then more. A whole pack of wolves slunk from the foliage, their fur bristling, their teeth bared.

Tercia's heart pounded. He raised the sharp stick defensively, his wounded leg shaking under the weight.

One wolf lunged forward, snapping its jaws inches from him. He swung the stick with all his strength, striking the beast across its muzzle. The wolf yelped but retreated only for a moment.

Another wolf darted at him from the side, its teeth grazing his arm. Tercia winced in pain but thrust the stick forward, pushing it back. His breath came in ragged bursts—he could not hold them off for long.

"Josia!" Joseph shouted desperately, his voice echoing through the forest.

For a moment, nothing happened. Then, with the sound of a thunderclap, a shadow leapt from the trees. Josia, the mighty jaguar, landed between the brothers and the wolves. His roar shook the very air, a sound filled with rage and dominance. His golden eyes blazed as if he had been waiting for this very battle.

The wolves snarled, circling warily, but Josia was faster, fiercer. With a blur of muscle and claws, he pounced on the lead wolf, pinning it down with crushing strength.

His jaws snapped shut, and the wolf cried out before falling silent. The pack hesitated, unsure. Josia's presence was overwhelming—an apex predator reclaiming his territory.

One by one, the wolves slunk back into the shadows, growling low but unwilling to face him again. The forest quieted, leaving only the sound of Joseph and Tercia's heavy breathing.

Joseph rushed to Tercia's side, steadying him. "Are you all right?"

Tercia nodded, though his arm throbbed from the bite. "I'm fine... thanks to Josia."

The jaguar padded toward them, his chest heaving, his fur streaked with sweat and rain. He rubbed his head against Joseph's shoulder, then against Tercia's hand, as if to say: *I told you I would never let harm come to you.*

When the camp finally fell quiet again, Josia stood panting, his fur slightly torn but his eyes still glowing with focus. Toseph limped over, blood on his jaw, but wagging his tail weakly.

The three of them stood together, stronger than ever, with Toseph watching from behind, barking proudly.

The sun began to sink, its golden light cutting through the mist.

The map said only a mile remained until the edge of the Amazon, where the world of men waited for them once more. They were battered, wounded, and weary—but united.

That evening, they walked on, their hearts lifted. With Josia at their side once again, nothing could stop them now.

Tomorrow, the jungle would release them.

Chapter 21
Something Shiny

The sun was gentle that morning, casting golden rays through the trees like a warm invitation. Joseph and Tercia had just finished organizing their supplies near their shelter, while Josia was relaxing nearby with his eyes half-closed and Toseph was busy sniffing around the base of trees like he was on a mission of his own.

It had been a quiet couple of days since they found the sword in the cave. That sword had stirred something in all of them—a sense that this place wasn't just wilderness, but a land hiding history. And possibly, secrets.

Joseph wiped his forehead and looked over at the wooden log where Eduardo had spent most of his time before vanishing. "Hey, Tercia," he called, "do you remember that Eduardo always used to sit there? Every day, same spot."

"Yeah," Tercia replied, tossing a stick into the campfire. "He said it had a 'nice view of the trees,' remember?"

Joseph chuckled, then walked toward the spot. Something about it had been nagging at him. He crouched down and inspected the area. The ground beneath the sitting spot looked a little... disturbed. Softer than usual.

Tercia joined him. "You thinking what I'm thinking?"

"Only one way to find out."

The boys grabbed their makeshift digging tools—flat stones and one of the wooden paddles they'd shaped into a mini-shovel. They started digging. The soil was loose and a bit sandy, like someone had once covered something up and patted it down quickly.

Only a few inches in, Joseph's shovel hit something solid. *Clink.*

"Whoa. Did you hear that?"

Tercia leaned closer and brushed away more dirt with his hands. A moment later, the sunlight reflected off something **golden**. Not yellow—**golden**.

They uncovered a **thick, rectangular bar**. Heavy. Shiny. Real.

Joseph held it in his hands and looked at Tercia. "Is this... is this gold?"

Tercia nodded slowly, speechless. "Looks like a gold bar."

Their hands trembled as they wiped the remaining dirt off it. There were faded letters on one side. Spanish. Maybe Portuguese.

"This had to belong to Eduardo," Joseph muttered. "Maybe this was part of the treasure his note talked about."

Instead of celebrating, both boys looked at each other, unsure. This wasn't just a cool discovery. It was part of a **legacy**, and part of a story they were now tangled in.

Just then, a sudden *rustle* in the leaves above made them jump.

Toseph barked excitedly and dashed toward a nearby tree, leaping and wagging his tail furiously. "Now what?" Tercia groaned, dusting his hands.

Joseph looked up. Hanging from a branch—snagged like it had been thrown years ago—was a **muddy, slightly deflated football**.

Tercia burst into laughter. "That's probably the most random thing we've found."

Toseph barked again, as if begging them to throw it already.

Joseph carefully climbed the lower branches and tugged it free. "It's not too damaged," he said, tossing it down.

The moment it hit the ground, Toseph pounced on it with pure joy, growling playfully and pushing it around like a trained striker. Joseph and Tercia watched, smiling for the first time that day.

"Imagine," Tercia said, "finding **gold and a football** in the same morning."

"Imagine hiding gold right under your sitting spot," Joseph added. "Eduardo must've been smarter than we thought."

Later that afternoon, they carefully cleaned the gold bar and stored it in a hidden compartment beneath the camp floor. They knew it was valuable—not just in terms of wealth, but what it **represented**. Proof of Eduardo's past. A piece of a puzzle that kept growing with each new discovery.

As for the football, it became Toseph's favorite toy. Even Josia gave it a nudge once or twice, though he preferred watching the younger hybrid chase it back and forth across the clearing.

That night, as they sat by the fire with Josia dozing near the flame and Toseph snoring beside the football, Joseph stared into the firelight and whispered, "We're in the middle of something big."

Tercia nodded. "And it all started with a seat... and something shiny underneath."

Chapter 22
First Sport of the Amazon

It had been days since the discovery of the gold bar and the football. The forest around them had slowly started to feel like a strange kind of home. With food sorted, shelter secured, and Josia and Toseph always by their side, Joseph and Tercia finally felt safe enough to do something they hadn't done since landing in the Amazon.

Have fun.

One late afternoon, as the sky turned orange and the air was thick with the scent of damp leaves, Tercia stood holding the slightly deflated football and smirked. "You thinking what I'm thinking?"

Joseph raised an eyebrow. "If you're thinking of football... then yes."

Tercia nodded. "Let's do it. Our first Amazon match."

The clearing next to their shelter was wide enough. A few sticks placed in the ground became makeshift goalposts. The ground was uneven, filled with roots and leaves, but they didn't care.

They assigned the teams:

- **Team Joseph**: Joseph and Josia.
- **Team Tercia**: Tercia and Toseph.

Neither of them were good at football, and both knew it. But that wasn't the point.

"Alright," Joseph said, dropping the ball in the center. "First to 3 goals wins."

Toseph barked and wagged his tail, already hopping around. Josia remained calm, crouched like a panther in position, his intense yellow eyes locked on the ball.

Tercia kicked off first. "Let's go!"

The ball rolled forward—bumpy and awkward over the forest floor. Toseph lunged, pawed it forward, and then headbutted it with surprising control. Joseph ran to block but slipped on a vine.

Before he could get up, *wham!*—Toseph nudged the ball into the goal.

"1-0!" Tercia shouted, pumping his fist.

Joseph groaned. "This is going to be embarrassing."

The second round was chaos. Josia, surprisingly fast, chased the ball with sleek movements. At one point, he leapt and batted the ball with his paw toward Joseph, who managed to guide it just enough to roll it into the goal.

"1-1!" Joseph shouted back, his face beaming with victory.

They kept playing—laughing, falling, cheering. Toseph ran circles around them, while Josia played with elegance and perfect timing. By the end, they were all covered in dirt and leaves, sweat dripping from their faces.

Eventually, Joseph's team won 3-2. But no one cared. They collapsed on the grass, breathing heavily, their stomachs hurting from laughing so much.

"Best sport ever," Tercia gasped, holding his ribs.

"In the middle of the Amazon," Joseph added. "With a jaguar and a dog-cat hybrid."

They all lay there, watching the sun slowly fade behind the canopy. Toseph rolled the ball back and forth between his paws. Josia sat upright, regal and proud.

It was their first sport in the Amazon, and they had created it entirely on their own.

As the light began to fade, Joseph stood up and walked toward where the ball had rolled into the bushes during the last goal. He bent to pick it up—but his hand brushed against **something cold and round** in the soil.

"What's this?" he muttered, brushing away some dirt.

It was a **coin**—old, with edges worn smooth and a faded symbol on one side. On the other side was an engraving: *1884*. Beneath it, the initials **E.C.M.** were just barely visible.

Tercia rushed over. "Is that... Eduardo's?"

Joseph nodded slowly. "Eduardo... something C... maybe his middle name?"

Tercia looked at it closely. "This might be one of his personal belongings."

Another piece of the puzzle. Another collectible for their chest of Eduardo's story.

They returned to the camp, placed the coin beside the sword, the note, and the gold bar, and looked at their growing collection.

That night, as the fire flickered, Joseph whispered, "We're not just surviving out here."

Tercia nodded. "We're discovering someone's entire life."

Chapter 23 The Final Days and A Secret of a Whole Life

The jungle had become their home. The rustling leaves, the smell of damp earth after rain, and the sound of strange creatures calling out at night—all of it had shaped their days and nights for what felt like a lifetime. But every adventure has its end, and Joseph and Tercia knew in their hearts that the time had come.

The morning sun filtered through the canopy, casting warm patches of light on their small camp. Joseph was quiet, sitting on a fallen log, staring at the horizon. Tercia, sharpening the edge of the forest-made axe they had crafted, noticed the distant look in his brother's eyes.

"You're thinking about it again, aren't you?" Tercia asked gently.

Joseph nodded. "Yes... It's time, Tercia. We've survived here, discovered things we never dreamed of, and even learned secrets buried for centuries. But we can't stay forever. The city calls us back."

Josia padded closer, pressing his head against Joseph's side as if sensing the gravity of the moment. Toseph, still playful as ever, barked lightly and pawed at the ground, but even he seemed to understand that something was changing.

That day, they laid out their plan.

From Eduardo's belongings, they had kept not only his letter but also the small clues he had left behind. Among them was a **map**, frayed and fragile, but still usable. The faded lines traced rivers, mountains, and hidden trails, all leading back toward civilization. It would be a long and dangerous journey, but it was possible.

Tercia studied the map carefully. "We'll need to travel by river for part of it. That's the fastest way out. Once we reach the high ridges, the city won't be far."

Joseph exhaled slowly, relief mixed with nervousness. "After all this time... the thought of hearing people again, walking on stone streets instead of mud—it almost feels unreal."

Josia growled softly at the mention of leaving, as if warning them that the jungle would never let go of its children so easily.

That evening, as the fire crackled and their last meal of roasted roots and herbs cooked, Joseph and Tercia made a final pact.

"We're not telling anyone about Eduardo," Joseph said firmly. His eyes glimmered in the firelight, filled with determination.

Tercia agreed without hesitation. "If the world learns what we know, it will destroy his legacy. People would dig up the jungle, tear it apart for treasure. Eduardo trusted us with his story. We keep it safe."

The flames danced, and the gold coin Eduardo had left them caught the light for just a moment, shining brighter than the rest of their belongings.

"One day," Tercia continued, lowering his voice, "we will come back. We'll follow the map, find the treasure, and honor Eduardo's life. But until then, the secret stays with us."

Josia lifted his head, eyes reflecting the fire like molten amber. Toseph wagged his tail and rested beside them. In that quiet moment, the two animals felt less like companions and more like guardians of the secret.

The next morning marked the beginning of their final days in the Amazon. They packed lightly—food, the map, Eduardo's sword and letter, and the collectibles they had stored. They left behind the farm, the bunker, and the memories carved into the trees.

As Joseph took one last look at their camp, he whispered, "This place gave us life when we had none. We owe it everything."

Tercia placed a hand on his brother's shoulder. "It's not goodbye forever. It's just... until we return."

And with that, the brothers, their jaguar, and their strange new companion began the long journey back to the city, carrying not just their belongings but the weight of a secret—a secret of a whole life, one that would shape their future and bind them forever to the heart of the Amazon.

Chapter 24
The Final Goodbyes

The day had come at last. Their belongings were packed, the map folded carefully inside Joseph's pouch, and the memories of the Amazon pressed heavily in their hearts. The morning air was heavy with dew, and mist hung low over the trees. The jungle, though alive as ever, seemed strangely quiet—as if it knew its children were leaving.

Joseph and Tercia stood side by side with Josia and Toseph. The jaguar's golden eyes flickered with sorrow, while Toseph pawed nervously at the ground, letting out small whines. Both animals had been more than companions; they had been brothers in the truest sense.

Joseph knelt down beside Josia, hugging the jaguar's strong neck. "We'll return," he whispered, his voice trembling. "I promise you, Josia. This isn't the end."

Tercia stroked Toseph's fur, tears in his eyes. "You've been with us through everything. Don't forget us. One day, when we come back, we'll find you here, waiting."

Josia pressed his head into Joseph's chest, and Toseph barked softly, his tail wagging weakly. The brothers stood, gave their final goodbyes, and turned toward the riverbank where their journey would begin. The animals remained behind, watching silently as Joseph and Tercia disappeared into the shadows of the trees.

The river was calm at first. Its gentle current carried them steadily downstream, the map guiding their way. The sound of the flowing water blended with the chorus of the rainforest, giving them courage. But by midday, the sky had grown dark, and clouds gathered above.

The first drops of rain were cool against their skin, but within minutes it turned into a storm. Sheets of rain poured down, drenching them in moments. The river, once steady, grew violent and rushed forward with terrifying force.

"Hold on!" Joseph shouted over the roar of the water.

Tercia, gripping the side of their makeshift raft, tried to steady himself. But a sudden surge sent him flying off the edge. With a cry, he plunged into the raging river.

"Tercia!" Joseph screamed, his heart nearly stopping.

The current dragged Tercia downstream, thrashing him against sharp rocks. He fought desperately to stay above water, but a jagged stone struck his leg, slicing it open. Blood mixed with the rain and river, and pain shot through him like fire.

Summoning every ounce of strength, Joseph leapt into the water. The cold shocked him instantly, but he swam hard, eyes locked on his brother. Just as Tercia began to sink, Joseph reached him, pulling him to the surface.

"Hold on, I've got you!" Joseph gasped, his arms burning as he fought the furious current.

After what felt like an eternity, Joseph managed to drag Tercia back to shore. Both collapsed on the muddy bank, gasping for air. Tercia clutched his leg, blood streaming down, but he was alive.

They knew they couldn't travel far that day. Joseph searched the ground until he found a sturdy branch—thick, strong, and straight. He snapped it into a walking stick and handed it to his brother.

"Here, lean on this. We'll make it together," Joseph said firmly.

Tercia nodded, his face pale but determined. He used the stick to support his weight, limping as they made slow progress along the riverbank.

By the time night fell, both were exhausted. Their clothes clung to their bodies, soaked through, and every step had been a struggle. They found a dry patch of ground beneath an overhanging rock where the rain couldn't reach. Joseph quickly built a small fire, its warmth pushing away the chill of the storm.

They ate quietly, their minds heavy with the day's events. Tercia stretched his wounded leg, pain etched on his face. Joseph sat close, watching the flames flicker.

"We're halfway there," Joseph said softly, trying to lift his brother's spirits. "Rest tonight. Tomorrow, we keep going."

Tercia managed a faint smile. "Halfway done... then we'll see the city again."

The rain softened into a steady drizzle, and the brothers lay side by side under the rock. The jungle's song played around them—the rustle of leaves, the distant cries of animals, and the steady rhythm of the river. For the first time in a long while, the future felt within reach.

Joseph and Tercia could hardly believe their eyes when the thick wall of trees finally parted, revealing the faint outline of civilization beyond. For months, the jungle had been their world—its dense canopy their sky, its rivers their roads, and its wild creatures their neighbors. Now, for the first time in what felt like forever, they saw the gray outlines of buildings, telephone poles, and the distant shimmer of lights.

But the escape was not without its struggles. Their bodies were weak, scarred, and battered from countless trials. Tercia's leg still throbbed from his fall into the river, and Joseph's shoulders ached from carrying much of their supplies.

Before they could step onto the dirt road ahead, a group of policemen and rescue workers appeared, their flashlights cutting through the misty air. Gasps and shouts echoed as the rescuers rushed forward. Joseph and Tercia were quickly surrounded, guided gently but firmly to safety.

"Bread," whispered Joseph as a warm loaf was pressed into his hands. He tore into it hungrily, the taste bringing tears to his eyes. Beside him, Tercia sipped hot chocolate, trembling as the warmth spread through his chest. These were things they had once taken for granted, but after surviving on fruits, roots, and wild game, they felt like luxuries beyond imagination.

At the hospital, doctors rushed to clean their wounds, bandage their cuts, and treat their exhaustion. "They're just boys," one nurse whispered, shaking her head in disbelief. Yet these boys had survived what most grown men could not.

Soon, reporters crowded outside, their cameras flashing as Joseph and Tercia were escorted out. Questions bombarded them—"How did you survive?" "What did you eat?" "Did you really fight off wolves?"—but the two friends only exchanged a look. They had lived through something the world would never truly understand.

Awards and medals soon followed. The mayor shook their hands. Scientists begged to hear about their discoveries. Collectors marveled at the artifacts they brought back. But beneath all the glory, Joseph and Tercia knew a truth no one else did: **Eduardo's treasure still lay hidden, waiting, deep within the Amazon.**

That night, lying in real beds with clean sheets, Joseph whispered to Tercia, "This isn't the end, you know."

Tercia nodded slowly, staring at the ceiling. "One day... we'll go back. For Josia, for Toseph, and for the treasure Eduardo left behind."

The boys closed their eyes, their hearts full of both relief and longing. They had escaped the Amazon, but the jungle would forever be a part of them. The story was not over—it was only the beginning of something greater.

About the Author

Abhiraj Gupta was born (2012) in Lucknow, Uttar Pradesh, India. He moved to Bangalore, Karnataka for schooling. He is fond of reading fiction books since early age and got inspiration of writing one his own. This is his first book and has no laurels up to date in the field of writing and literature, but he plans to earn those.

Stay tuned for future books!! : -)